Lines in the Sand

First published in Great Britain in 2024 by Dithering Chaps
on behalf of the Bournemouth Writing Festival

Copyright © individual authors, 2024

ISBN: 978-0-9574538-5-2

Printed in Great Britain on recycled paper by Imprint**Digital**
(made from FSC® Recycled certified post-consumer waste pulp)

Cover design by Briony Hartley of Goldust Design
www.goldustdesign.co.uk

Dithering Chaps would like to dedicate this chapbook to everyone who entered the competition and to the supportive writing community it created

Foreword   *by Dominic Wong, Festival Director*

Since the Bournemouth Writing Festival's conception at the end of 2022, I have been overawed by the positivity and openness of the writing community, not just here on the South Coast of England, but also across the United Kingdom and beyond.

The first Bournemouth Writing Festival in April 2023 started something much bigger than the 70+ writing events and activities that were put on over a three-day weekend. Writers, authors and writing professionals from across the country and abroad came to our town, and met and mingled with other like-minded people. Our visitors were inspired by the diverse and varied programme they attended and the longstanding association that Bournemouth has with great literary figures.

Inspired by the likes of Mary Shelley, JRR Tolkien and Robert Louis Stephenson – to name just three – Bournemouth is fast becoming a place of creativity, stimulus and encouragement for writers of all abilities and backgrounds, thanks to the kindness and inclusivity of those involved.

The Festival – and its subsequent networking events and online community – has created a tangible atmosphere of inspiration to encourage writers at all stages of their writing journey to get those words flowing and ignite a passion for prose.

This anthology – our first – shines a light on the incredible range of writing. Drawing on our seven miles of sandy beaches for our theme of *Lines in the Sand*, we've been overwhelmed by the quality, diversity and talent that came from just four simple words.

We were delighted to welcome underrepresented writers into the competition, working with fantastic local community arts groups who strive to give a platform to those living on the edge of society. Indeed, the donations from entrants to this competition raised hundreds of pounds for Vita Nova – a charity based in Bournemouth that encourages recovering addiction writers to express themselves and find purpose. As the world becomes more fractured, it is important to hear everyone's voice.

As an author myself, I know that writing can be a lonely business. Sat behind your laptop, stewing over each word or metaphor and waiting for those sales to trickle in, sometimes you need a bit of help, guidance and cheerleading. So, I was lucky to be able to call upon local publisher Dithering Chaps, our two judges, Natalie Scott and Charlotte Fodor from the Arts University, and industry experts, Briony Hartley (cover design) and Linda Liebrand (marketing support). I thank them all for their outstanding contributions.

That's just the tip of the iceberg. The positivity that has grown out of the Bournemouth Writing Festival has made those in our writing community a little less lonely. Knowing other writers are out there and have your back can make your writing journey so much more joyful.

Your words have power but so do your actions. Join in. Take part. Raise your hand. Be kind and supportive and listen to as many different voices as you can. Because you never know what journey others are on.

But above all, keep writing – we need to hear your unique story, and your voice deserves to be heard.

I hope you enjoy this anthology and join our Writing Festival community soon.

Our Poetry Judge

Natalie is a lecturer across all units of the BA (Hons) Creative Writing course and Module Leader for the MA in Creative Writing, due to start in May at Arts University Bournemouth

Dr Natalie Scott

It's been a privilege and a delight to judge the poetry competition. Poets responded to the theme of *Lines in the Sand* in many diverse and interesting ways. Some chose to explore it literally, using the beach as a setting to describe physical marks made in the sand. Many poets touched on the ephemeral nature of lines such as these and it led to some thought-provoking symbolic interpretations. Others approached the topic metaphorically, within very different contexts but where there were lines to be crossed. Here there was an exploration of subject-matter that included significant milestones in life, journeys of experience, crossing into death, breaking the rules, with echoes of themes such as identity, relationships and change.

It was very close at the top end of the competition and choosing the final twenty poems was tough. In the end I was drawn to the most memorable poems, in their choice and presentation of subject-matter, in their ability to shock, move, amuse, challenge, provoke, and in the way they left some part of the world changed for me upon their reading. Congratulations to all the winners and thank you for sharing your words with me.

Natalie's web page: www.nataliescottwriter.com
Natalie on Twitter/X: @NatalieAnnScott
Natalie's staff page: https://staff.aub.ac.uk/en/profile/natalie-scott

Our Flash Fiction Judge

Charlotte is a Creative Writing Lecturer at Arts University Bournemouth, where she teaches the following short courses:

1. Creative Writing – An Introduction

2. Memoir and Autofiction Writing

Charlotte Fodor

I thoroughly enjoyed reading and evaluating the flash fiction entries, each offering a unique perspective on the theme of *Lines in the Sand.* The process of reviewing these flash fiction pieces was both enlightening and inspiring, highlighting the creativity and artistry that can be conveyed through storytelling, especially when writing is contained to a strict word count as demanded by flash fiction.

The variety of interpretations of *Lines in the Sand* within these stories showcases the depth and complexity of human experiences. The authors have masterfully crafted narratives that captivate and engage. The winning pieces exemplified the important elements of flash fiction: language, unsaid nuances, tight prose, and resonance. The stories left an indelible impression, lingering in my mind long after the initial read. Thank you, writers. It was a privilege to read every one of your stories.

Charlotte's webpage: https://thecharlotteweb.wordpress.com/about/
Charlotte Twitter/X: @thecharlotteweb

Contents

I Witness Creation

by Robin Muers

The deity – maybe five or six –
marks out a wonky circle
with her spade.
What's inside it - a mussel shell,
a scrap of bladderwrack,
a plastic cow – get names and jobs.
Her word gives life and lots to do.

The granddad blunders in
to video the scene. Quite wrong:
two feet in trainers
smudge the edge of a universe.
The pulse of *then and then and then*
that drove the cosmos on
dies from interruption.

Cheese Sandwich

by Neil Douglas

Wear a black dinner suit, an ochre cummerbund, silk, which picks up the red hue of the dunes. Wear an emerald bow tie, undone, limp around your neck below a cliff-edge jawline as the director demands a languid demeanour to suggest it is ennui rather than ambient temperature that is killing you. This is high-end fragrance.

The voiceover quotes Nietzsche, a smokey French accent – *when you gaze long into an abyss, the abyss also gazes into you.*

You must wait for Salvation to shimmer over your horizon – all gauzy billow in a white shift, 6-inch heels, legs up to ya-ya. Beside Salvation, flown in from Mexico, the obligatory ocelot on a diamante leash, whiskering the dry air with slight disinterest.

But Salvation is nowhere to be seen.

Your hunger bites. Lean against a phallic rock. Pierce the distance with impossibly blue eyes. Behind the rock, sweating in its plastic wrapper, a cheese sandwich.

How the Dressmaker of Bournemouth Feeds her Family

by Alice E. Bennett

There were 27-and-a-half starfish above the counter of the fancy dress shop. The cranberry-coloured one, the biggest and spikiest of them all, broke apart when a previous customer tried to rip it off, leaving three shrivelled limbs and a white space where the other two used to be. This was what the shopkeeper told me, as she ran her needle in and out of a piece of fabric across her knee.

Bournemouth was a town alien to me, my first and only visitation the result of a sketchy friendship and the odd Christmas card whenever memory served me. I skirted my fingertips along the range of outfits; after this weekend there would be no more trips to the coast, where the sea spray stings your eyes and grains of sand itch between your toes.

'Nothing taking your interest, dear?' the shopkeeper asked, her voice creaking in time with the floorboards overhead.

I lifted a hanger from one of the busy railings. Long, thin and green, the item looked like it intended to transform the wearer into seaweed. I caught the shopkeeper staring. 'Not my size,' I muttered, and pushed it back into place.

She never introduced herself by name, the shopkeeper, despite the overfamiliarity in her voice and the playful dexterity which she applied to her craft. She drew a length of cotton from her pocket and bit down, violently snapping the thread.

'The occasion?' she asked through gritted teeth, eyes down.

'Hen-do. Apparently, I missed the memo on the theme, so here I am.'

The shopkeeper looked up from her lap. 'You're not from around here, are you?'

'That obvious?'

She smiled. 'Your octopus legs are falling off.'

I refastened the safety pins around my belt, cheeks reddening. 'I assumed fancy dress meant wearing a joke costume.'

Outside the shop the sun was setting, a blood-red sky fading into the dark ripples of the English Channel. 'How much for the navy two-piece in the window?'

The shopkeeper slipped her fingers into an old cardboard box at the base of her chair, retrieving a pot of glue and a golden starfish. Coated in a crust of multicoloured gems, the starfish sparkled in the fading light, as the sun dipped below the sea.

'Depends,' she replied as she began applying a thin ribbon of glue to its pale underbelly. 'How much do you want to get out of that outfit?'

Ghost Crabs

by Laurie Keim

After the night wind, a blank slate.
On the bare sand, the ghost crabs
touch the world so lightly
they must renew their identity
each morning in ancient script.

Georgic

by Partridge Boswell

In the milk-eye of a dying ewe, unfathomable sky. Crouched in mudshit straw

you cradle her neck while the young vet eases a syringe under her shoulder

and cries—an unconditional friend for life. Her dun fleece recedes past men,

pausing at the woods' far edge. The river shadows a train's bent moan

threading the valley below. Come spring you'll find her bleached bones

scattered like signs by coydogs in the back pasture, your first lesson in

the futility of burial. You were new to this too, learning what earth preordained

and what would grow or fade with neglect—from damp leaves under an outcrop,

defiant tines of horsetails—or else the hard art of noticing without grieving:

paddock superseded by burdock and thistle, rats that scurried from sweet feed

bins at the barn door's roar to hide in old bales, molasses warm on their breath.

If a mud-matted ruminant has a soul, how not a man? How did you watch a single

hawk carry away an entire flock of cochins and imagine you wouldn't be

devastated and revived by soulful and soulless alike, saints and scum hanging

thick as webs of haydust from the rafters? Tossing and stacking the loft, load after load in hundred-degree heat, sweat-drenched skin plastered with

dried grains and motes of clover and timothy, then sitting on porch steps at dusk

while kids build and defend castles of hay, amnesty of burnt arms and necks—

nothing more needing to be lifted beyond the G major resonance of muscle at rest.

The land lingers suspended in benediction. The homeless come home with the same

dream they lit out with slung over their shoulder, scuffed and worn but unchanged

as the eyes of an old friend you assumed you'd never live to see again.

Between garden, flock and field of rocks, what was it you were farming exactly?

Everything else the runoff takes with it come spring, leaching down to the lees

of a manure-fed cattail pond, where rumour has it the pope once swam

naked as the sun when he was the schoolmate of neighbours from

the old country. Before he was the pope, before he was anyone.

Castle

by Craig Smith

Below the necklace of seaweed, we stake out a real estate
of bare sand, where my son and I build.

A moat, a metre across and a hand deep.
The excavated sand becomes the castle.

We beachcomb a portcullis of razor shells, dog whelks
for battlements, mussel shells as tracing, as ornamentation.

This is good sand, damp, clingy, tactile.
The calm sea will soon destroy our work.

This February light is astounding. The warmth, this winter teatime,
is unnatural. We cannot justify removing our shirts, but we do.

We have burned more than we should burn, spilled
more than we should spill, but we are swathed in gold.

We cut a gully from the castle to the ocean's edge.
Our fingertips graze stones and shells buried by yesterday's tide.

We log the patterns of the sea: the bigger waves
that make the incursion; the milder waves that putter in their wake.

The boy skims stones; the ocean, like a dog,
returns them to his feet.

A Converse All Star washes by.
The boy retrieves it, drops it above the high waterline.

The dike we built to baffle the sea is breached at the outer edge.
The flood begins there.

We cheer when the two hands of water meet,
like arms embracing our work.

The sea erodes the castle base, the shoddy infrastructure,
the lack of foundations. Fissures widen with each new wave.

Our neighbours shore up their defences.
For each rebuilt bulwark, the water finds a fresh ingress.

We retreat inland, to the pavilion,
to mooch to our Airbnb, to tweet our friends.

Woman standing on her bathroom scales

by Carol Maxwell

The lines
Are so small
Need to get my glasses
My optometrist appointment is due
Will need more snap fastener extensions
Packs of three on eBay for fifteen dollars
Hip flexors, must restart home Pilates
Turtle belly, pot calling turtle
Gotta bend at the hips
Once it hits seventy-five
That'll kill off the wine
Definitely moving to vodka
Need to redo my toe nail polish
Something poppy summery bright
Sunflower yellow or orange maybe
Oil, put oil on the shopping list
Ok, calling it at seventy-five
Gagging for a coffee
Do I need a shave?
Had a pee
Naked as
Here we go
No way!
Darn it!
The open
Pinot Gris!
Phone SJ
She'll help
Seventy-six
Definitely, seventy-six it is

No Matter Which Way the Wind Blows

by Charles Kitching

A solid wooden ruler manufactured by Garricks of Brighton. A twelve-inch straight edge, not chipped nor splintered by time. "Made in England" proudly embossed upon its spine, sitting neatly beside his blotter. A present from his father, bought for a son nervously being sent off to board at Harrow, all those years ago. It came with a beautifully stencilled tin, containing set-squares, a protractor, steel compasses and slide-rule. The scene upon its lid showed the rolling Sussex downs where he'd roamed freely as a child, flying kites, birdwatching, and trainspotting.

As he sits at his grand mahogany Whitehall desk, he feels his father's spectral hand on his shoulder, saying "Bravo son", as he plots out 'peace' across maps of the fallen Ottoman Empire. His father had been a proud man, a staunch advocate of the British Empire's 'morality'. Yet he was glad his father had not witnessed the horrific carnage the previous years had brought, tearing the world apart, especially his beloved France, but that was all over now.

He'd not served on the front himself; his civil-service role exempting him from being mobilized. Two years had passed since the guns fell silent, although Spanish influenza and supporting the White Russians against the Bolshevik "red scourge" still took their toll. Needing no further deliberation regarding land he'd learnt was but vast tracts of desert, he laid his sturdy ruler upon the map and drew a firm straight line.

Another car bomb rips through more civilian neighbour-hoods. Her fragile home rocks; walls crumbling. She must flee. American soldiers are rounding up anyone and everyone. You can see first-world oil lust in their shameless eyes. Multiple infighting militias are spreading unrest mercilessly. She grabs a photograph as she runs to seek refuge. Pausing briefly, she looks at the faded sepia image, taken by a Scottish infantryman ninety years ago. It shows her grandparents and her mother as a baby. They'd been a nomadic people then, a noble people whose lives were bounded by the winds alone, governed by the stars, ruled by intuition's sense of seasons, an imbued awareness of shifting sands over which they'd roamed freely for countless generations, far back into pre-history. Their camel trails had known no borders, understood no concept of "state", until lines were drawn, overnight, upon paper, with a ruler, by someone they never knew nor who'd ever come here to learn about them.

Weather House

by Helen Jane Campbell

I had burst out into the hallway just before the storms started. And I'd been standing in position for several weeks.

My wooden counterpart, Gretel, is employed exclusively to herald sunshine, while I fanfare oncoming rain. It's an unusual job share, steeped in tradition and rigid rules.

I usually relish my role. Since this recent bout of storms though, well, I'd begun to sense Gretel was missing out. It had poured for two weeks straight and she'd been so cooped up. I hesitate to admit it, but I longed for her quiet company.

So, while lightning struck the Dorset clifftops in the distance, I pictured us no longer separated by mechanisms and carpentry, no longer silent and unacquainted. As forks of light shattered the sky, I imagined reaching into the dark warmth of the little weather house behind me, boldly taking Gretel's hand and releasing us both from the shackles of our carved abode.

My imagination ran riot with dreams of adventure, yet my body was stuck on sentry duty until the forecast changed.

Of course, I'd have lost everything if, in my attempts, I'd toppled off this wooden porch. I imagined in horror the repercussions. Yet the storms had emboldened me: the sky itself was dancing and I felt its electricity.

Thunder seemed to vibrate the entire building and flashes lit up our hallway like a Christmas tree. I imagined an illicit escape, right out into the tempestuous world itself, to enjoy gusty beaches and bursting clouds. And – if willing to join me – I pictured how Gretel's enigmatic presence could further illuminate the magical evening.

Hand-in-hand we'd explore the vast beach for the first time ever. One single night of indulgence, fuelled by a storm, until, when dawn broke, well, of course then our responsibilities would call us back up to the house, to resume our familiar roles and positions in the hallway. Standing proudly, either end of our balance bar, our days would, once again, be dictated by humidity. Locked in perpetual symbiosis. The lines we'd danced into the sand, washed away.

My reverie broke. The thunder had quietened and the rain had eased. A warm early morning glow rose in the hallway and I began to move, slowly backwards, finally on my familiar route home. I caught sight of Gretel emerging, stoic and elegant as always, ready to predict a clement day.

To My Future Ex-Husband, With Love

By Julia Rapp

When the cypress reaches its arms over the highway
it has a vinyl balloon caught in its branch like a sperm
snagged on a female condom, and I wonder what kind
of single mother I will be. Probably one that pours wine
in the unrinsed coffee mug from last morning and gags
on the first sip and thinks aloud *at least it tastes better
than dick*. I don't have a child. If one was strapped
in the booster seat behind me I'd talk to her like an adult,
using words like *existential crisis* and she'd tie my hair
back with her little doughy hands when I've had too many.
I'm not a drunk. My future ex-husband will tell you differently.
He's a gentle soul — the kind of person you can trust, but
I never did. So, it'll be me and baby Patricia. On her birthday
I'll take her to the coast in Pacifica. We'll release balloons
to the heavens in a reverse hailstorm and I'll whisper:
See? On a clear day, you can see up God's skirt.

Blue Hospital Gown

by Kim Waters

Your blood count low, your kidneys in strife,
fluid flowed over your lungs like a waterslide
as you lay on a fluidized air-bed repeating
the last things we said and confusing the words
up and down. You couldn't remember the taste
of food or how you'd come to be lying there,
an oxygen mask covering your mouth. You
wanted to walk out of your blue hospital gown
and swim, once again, in the Yarriambiack Creek.
You wanted to be a girl in a green velvet dress,
smoking a cigarette and sipping a shandy. There
seemed no way to stop you sliding into the past,
but at the last moment you dug in your heels
and bum-shuffled your way back to the start.

Might Love End Life

by Henry Edwards

On the rock-hard mattress rests your frail, massive wreck,
fixed and straight. I clip your toe nails, hold your slender
feet and wipe off the flaky skin. 'Dorset grit, Betty. Nothing
to be ashamed of!' you'd say. Now silence fills the air. No
more the sand from neath the pier, but duvet dust and linen
grime.

I wash your thin legs, lift shrivelled, feeble arms, lifeless, all
muscles withered. What'll I do with you now, Jack, what
now? Your shoulders, white and bony, the source of
boundless strength, twirling me in the cold green Channel,
burying me in the sands, dressing me with shells, lifting me
in celebration, throwing me onto the bed, tossing the kids in
the air, stomping and laughing on the lawn, hand-in-hand
our put-the-world-to-rights walks by the Bourne, mourning
our folks and cheering your teams, my arms were always
too short, you were so big and so bubbly. And now? What
now Jack?

Breathing of this world, yet passed away. Cleaning,
feeding, washing to conceal decay, the stench, the towels,
the months of stillness, endless hygiene. I am but a
cantilever, shifting ever further from that solid pillar of
devotion and intimacy to keep a balance; beneath me
stretches open space, a void, nothing. If I'm honest, Jack, I
don't think I can handle this anymore. I'm tired. I'm so tired.

'All blood levels normal, pressure OK, 140 over 70, nothing
to worry about, pulse calm as ever,' says the nurse.

'And where is Jack?" I ask. Her hand on my shoulder tells
volumes, and then she's gone. In truth: all are so kind; grief
and suffering trigger compassion.

You've crawled into the carapace I disinfect; your impish grin will not return. The blackbird from childhood with broken wing flashes through my mind; the waiting, feeding, hoping, before I placed a cloth over its head and snapped its neck.

What now Jack? I have the needle ready. In the garden stalks a crow, they've nested in the chimney. Instinct tells me hope is lost. Might love end life? The crow, shiny black on bright lawn green, stares at me with beady eyes. We think it's time, Jack. We think it's time.

Paul Klee Said, 'Take a Line for a Walk'

by Roger Hare

it
complained we only
ever went familiar ways – I tried to explain.
Instead, it took the lead in quiet, comforting curves:
swirls of a musical key: a jagged fall down stairs: as a filament
unswerving enough to leave the Earth, join stars together, have me
guess at shapes. For a while we came to an understanding,
marked out a playing-field each day, but the line had
life beyond the rules, drew attention to its siblings
in the sand, said, *I'm not like them, don't expect
me to agree.* I felt its days of growing
strain, it's want to stretch in ways
I wouldn't follow. Its final
slipping of my grasp
left me to watch as
it became the
the tail of
a kite, a
flicker
in the
wind
a
s
c
e
n
d
i
n
g

(The title comes from a quote by artist Paul Klee: '… A drawing is simply a line going for a walk.')

On Hilbre Island, West Kirby

by Helen Kay

When the Triassic waves shaped Hilbre
       they made a playground for flowers
that sip a poet's sun.
   A giggle of bird's foot trefoil lights up
      sandstone layers,
waves a warm welcome to the skitter of visitors.
Clumps of sea thrift skip
        across the mossy grass to spectate
bobbles of grey seals.
   Cheered on by the wind,
the flowers dance in confidence
        that when the tide creeps away
    the visitors will paddle back
across the ridged lines of sand
    their feet reading a braille of shells.
They will feel their cheeks glow
    and the taste of salty pink flowers
       will hang on their tongues.

Changeling

by Helen Chambers

I turn from the bonfire's spit and crackle and limp down the
beach to the sea. No one watches. Not Mother, Father, nor
my sisters. They whoop and laugh and sing, caught up in
the excitement of the Midsummer Beach party.

Disentangling my floral crown from my frizzy hair, I wrist-
flick it back to the tide-line, where a herring gull swoops and
pecks. Jagged sound and movement still rasp in my head. I
never remember the aimless words and complex actions,
despite my littlest sister's patient rehearsing. I wish for
Mother's elegance and co-ordination, for her blonde hair
and indigo eyes. I wish I looked like my family.

Splashing into the shallows, I gasp at the cold then relax
into its embrace. I'm still wearing Mother's old grey dress,
the one she lent me, saying I was ready. It doesn't look
much on me. She said it'd make me light and delicate, and
she's right. I swim, weightless. My legs power me the way
they cannot on land. My ineptitudes sluice away. The sea's
a slippery ally, but I read her moods. I swim for my favourite
rocky outcrop, planning to doze in the warm sunrise,
beached like a seal, far from the noisy party.

I'm barely half-way when the other music starts.

From the sea, but not of the sea.

The sound of winter's sky: flashes of rubies, emeralds and
sapphires shimmering. Waterfalls bubble and laugh, silver
ripples up and down my spine: the salt breeze; the lazy
evening sea; a deep premonition of something shifting.

Looking back over my shoulder, the sea is orange-flamed shattered glass. Ahead, it's tranquil with music.

I swim in rhythm and beach upon my rock. Peering over the lee side of the outcrop, people dance, hidden. Different people, different dancing.

These folk are like me, with ropes of copper hair. Stocky people, who stomp, spin and splash. One spots me, smiles, beckons, reaches out with damp hands. Green eyes like mine.

I join them. No aches, no pain, no limping. We whirl and shimmy, twist and turn. Maybe minutes, maybe hours, until the haunting music fades. Each takes up a shawl of grey which glimmers with starlight, and they melt into the dark sea.

My mother's dress, fine as gossamer and dusted with dawn light, silks smoothly. My first watery breath refreshes me. The seals wait and I flow to them.

Island Seeker

by Antoine Cassar

Walking through the city
you're at it again
scouring for islands
in an ocean of stone

Oil stains
peeling walls
clumps of powder
dot-to-dot
holes to grasp onto
voids to fill seconds with
shapes to give life to
archipelagoes of possibility

And as usual
you haphazardly drift
toward the shore

Where All the Vibrators Go

by Tessa Foley

Who loves the now unmittened one?
faithful, dumb beneath the 'tress,
mm-murmuring one last kindly cum,
new turning heads are turning heads
for bunny glossy-pink in print.

Groping under pastel sheets
fingers eaten whole by valance,
unbalanced now – there's two!
Two true and darling rubber loves,
choice of which will thee engulf.

So take the latest one to heart,
start at one of seven speeds,
but the first one lurks amongst the reeds -
where does it go and does it think of me?

Guilty thoughts of discarded love as filler
for the compost box, Oh yes
all for keeping strictly ecological but where
do you recycle disused ersatz cocks?

Vag-me-downs for charity shops?
It's not its fault - this stops
and bucks and fasts with me,
I am the refusing queen.

Some other - she may need it now,
though boiling wouldn't be enough.
And best that we don't keep in touch.

Cross wibbling legs and pray to God
that all the jelly veins degrade
deep beneath the veggie patch.

A Fishy Tale

by David Longstaff

Dog walkers. It's always dog walkers that find bodies. Well, not this time. Another wave crashes behind me and I exhale and pull, trying to keep a steady rhythm. In the early morning light, her tail fin draws dark lines in the sand measuring our slow progress.

I look over my shoulder at the retreating tide and my heel slips, both legs shoot forward and I land hard on the base of my spine. The mermaid slumps against my chest and her mobile slides onto the wet sand. It shimmers and an iridescent shine illuminates another new message; Are you ok? I Love you xxx. I retrieve the phone, there isn't time to explain, she needs to be in the water. I wriggle out from under her, stagger to my feet and curl my arms around her torso. Another wave crashes behind me and I start dragging again. Stooped over and twisting from side to side I keep hauling her backwards toward the sea.

My feet splash in the shallow foam and my boots fill with water. Tiny stones swirl beneath me and the beach seems to tilt sideways. I drop to one knee, dizziness and nausea flood my body but I keep pulling. An icy hand slaps against the back of my head and we tumble forward, rolling over each other in the surf. I scramble to my hands and knees. Long strands of salty saliva hang from my lips. Her phone continues to pulse. I rip it from my pocket and read the message; Have you told him yet? How did he take it? Please reply! xxx. I throw the phone further up the beach, roll the mermaid over and drag her into the inky water.

Another wave crashes around us. My body is shaking and my jaw is snapping at the cold air. The water swirls around my knees and the mermaid starts to drift. With clenched fists, I grab the fabric and steer her around trying to push her away from the shore and out to the sea. Something slaps the water next to me. No. No. No. This cannot be happening! A dog, its teeth clamped around a corner of her tail and a man shouting from the shore.

"Mate, what's in the bag?"

"Get your dog under control," I scream back.

He wades in reaching for the mermaid. "What's in the sleeping bag!"

Rising

by Joanna Bury

Can you pass me the water?

The container is bobbing just out of reach. He nudges it
towards me. I know what he's thinking, why didn't we leave
when we could? I suppose you could say it's a protest. Not
like those protests they used to do, gluing yourself to
something or blocking a road, no nothing stupid like that.
This is a serious protest. We're not leaving our house until
the fire brigade agrees to pump it out. In fact I'm staying
right here in my lounge.

They were at the balcony in one of their little boats earlier,
kitted out like the army. Maybe they were the army? I told
them to sling their hook. Their hook. Do you get it? They're
in a boat and I'm telling them to … oh never mind. The
bottom line is I'm not leaving. Do they know how much this
house is worth? I've lived here a good twenty years. It's on
a sand spit. Try saying that without spitting, just a little. Go
on. My lips purse and the final consonant tingles the tip of
my tongue.

What? He's swimming near me.

Nothing, I reply.

Anyway, it's a peninsula, a line of sand stretched out into
the sea or the bay or the harbour or whatever. I could give
you all the details but right now I've got other things on my
mind because they're back, the fire brigade or the army or
whoever they are. They've bobbed back onto our balcony in
their little bobbing rubber boat.

This is your last chance, says the one sitting in the front.
She reaches out her hand.

He swims towards me. Come on, he says, it's time to go.
He tries to smile encouragingly but his face is just too sad.

Oh all right, I say.

My teeth are chattering, it's true.

They haul us up, wrap us in blankets and we float across
the balcony. Outside is nothing but sea. All around us. Sea.

Come on lads, paddle, says the one in charge.

They're paddling like mad but the coast is nowhere in sight.
The jumble of roofs and drifting rubbish where the sand spit
used to be is getting further and further away.

He looks old and cold and miserable. I take his hand.

I told you we should have stayed in the lounge, I say.

Tango

by Michael Pettit

I peer at an image of a sculpture fashioned from eyebrow hairs. The hairs are glued tip to tip with phlegm. The artist's name is [;]. I ponder this and the notion of fragility.

I'm distracted as a woman passing by steps up to the wall of magazines. Her silk scarf, fixed with a brooch, signals taste and power. Her hair sculpts expensive space around the years that line her face. Hauteur is honed, a dab on a pulse point here and there. Magazines pimp and preen: ultra everything. Her eye swans over them. A man – grey, pink, groomed – comes up quietly behind her and, with a tiny smile, places his hands in a tender proposition on her waist. Her flinch is the twitch of a clock hand, as irrevocable. It is a line drawn in the sand. She reaches for a magazine. Grey, pink, still as a chair he stands. Two beats. He adjusts his stance a calibrated degree away from her. Six beats. Then his shape gives, something crucial slackens, and he stands – white trousers, crisp shirt – bereft on a promontory.

It's a choreography of exactitudes, bare and eloquent as Japanese Noh, a secret language quarried over time to finesse the dark and communicate the unspeakable. I dare not look away.

At the perfect moment the woman returns to her husband's side, parallel bodies in terrible affinity. A dense silence – of perfect duration – accommodates, enables, directs, and they step forward and move grimly through the bookshop like shell-shocked survivors crossing an ashen battlefield, and out into the mall's bright, marbled avenue. A moment later, their bodies shake off and realign to renew an old conspiracy of compromise, and conversation starts up. Coupled, they head off to a movie, a restaurant, or perchance another interment.

I return to [;]. Another eyebrow artwork, this one suspended from a frame of phyllo pastry.

The Crescendo at Blue Beach, Gaza

by Elliot Chester

The phosphorus fog hovers like a wraith over the beach.
Shells litter the sand, but not the sort you may think.
There's nothing I'd make arts and crafts from, no intricate
rivets I'd score my fingernails over, nothing I'd cup to my
ears and hear the Gazan ocean, deftly hissing. I've
befriended tinnitus from the recent street bombing;
shrapnel severed my spinal cord, which left me paralysed.
Household items propelled outwards, upwards, downwards.
The power of the bomb was so immense—bricks crumbled
like meringue, but there's nothing flavoursome about this
scene; this desolate place. I turn my head back; admiring
lines in the sand from my wheelchair. They're always
parallel, no matter how uneven the setting. I'm drawn to a
lifeguard's chair with its amputated leg, beheaded palm
trees in gloopy soil, and mattresses promoting metal
dreams, where no one ever sleeps. I prise a parasol stick
from blood splattered rubble and find a patch not tinted red.
I etch the first line. I'll make my own sheet music, a short-
lived symphony which I hope's understood, if only by
waves. An army of lines follow suit. I add the first symbol;
the *accent*, meaning emphasised by stress or touch,
followed by double *f*'s, a raucous *fortissimo*. A couple of
slurs next—fitting—that transition should be smooth.
Unlikely. I etch two *staccatos*, it's time these were elected,
the status of these? Distinct. Disconnected. I conjure up the
staffs, representing different pitches, octaves of screams;
shrieks; pleas? Let's not forget the *triplets*; three victims for
the price of two; snuggled up, followed by a *half rest*. A
lengthy pause. Interval. The sarcasm of *dim* symbols,

fading gradually in loudness? The irony. *Treble* and *bass clefs* now attack the last line, followed by an *F* on each side, just because they look like ears. Deafness. But can you hear an unsung anthem, can you decode this mish-mash; this mania? My legs twitch. A sensory moment. I uprise from my chair, aghast—my arms and legs splayed. I stumble, then walk; ditching the stick in the ocean, that's definitely a *flat*, sinking. Finally, the crescendo builds and builds—as the white noise of war ensues. I'm the conductor; sketching the most relevant symbols of them all, using only my feet. The *whole rest*. The *time signature*. *Repeat*.

Body Found on Seafront

by Georgina Titmus

Graffitied sand. *NO VACANCIES*
Victoriana. He's missed the last bus—

home.

He fears their steps like-a-beat-like-a-drum.
Like a *danse macabre*

tattoo.

The streetlamp's Machiavellian
glow,

mimics
       sanctuary.

[Untitled]

by Dave Martin

Infinite white salts
By turns growl over hot sand
Etching on fine grain

Unstuck

by Cristín Leach

After the seaweed bath, she found a tiny mollusc
clamped to the inside of her left labia. A slight itch
alerted her to its presence. And then, reaching down
inside her pants as she walked on the beach, a smooth
lump where no lump had been. A small, hard surface on
moveable skin; a round bump beneath the pad of her
fingerprint. It was strange, but everything was now. And
so, she took it on board as another unexpected
discomfort, a surprise, but not fully a mystery, arriving
neat and slightly itchy at the end of four years of
unexpected things.

They had come to this hotel at the edge of the Atlantic
Ocean, Ireland-side, to be near the sea and, she had
supposed, each other. Five years ago, still married. She
remembered then as she felt the curve of the sudden
lump tight to her skin, that he had said to her, it's your
fault. It's your fault we don't fit. And she wondered at
how certain accusations stuck and played like a record
jumping back to repeat each time the needle hit a
scratch. Memories were like a wave from the ocean,
different each time one repeated because she was
different now, and the same because here again was a
crest she had felt before, born of the same water. You
are the reason this marriage won't work, he said. You
are unbending. She accepted that. Took it for an
unassailable fact.

Standing still by the water, her fingernail slid under the thin, translucent shell as she detached it, so delicate. Revealed in the grey afternoon light, it was pale yellow with thin turquoise lines radiating up and over the dome, outside. Inside, its body withdrew, gathering itself into itself again for protection. A baby blue-rayed limpet. A fragile, still beginning of a thing. Blown from her fingertip by the wind, it followed her gold wedding band into the ocean. The end.

And she thought about how it had unexpectedly survived the drying out and processing, held its breath at the moment of vacuum packing, and floating revived was born again among the too-hot sliming fronds of rehydrated kelp at the spa, before finding a shore to cling to: her body. Her body, a short-term travel companion, deeply mismatched, an intimate stranger to point those electric blue lines back to the sea and deliver them both home, unstuck.

Harvest of Things

by Oonagh Montague

She stole things.
"Don't leave things about for her to take." I was told.
What kinds of things I wondered. My mother said her friend
had something called kleptomania, which meant she took
things that weren't hers. This meant I was to "be careful". I
didn't understand how to do that, since I didn't have a lock on
my door and anyway, what would a grown lady want with the
things I had? This knowledge I had of her created an uneven
dynamic where her adultness felt like an illusion, like she was
something other than autonomous, victim to her wandering
hands, spasms of involuntary pilfering. It led me that first night
to breach the privacy of her room as she sat downstairs,
something I would never have thought to do, but her adulthood
felt cracked open, assailable. I opened her suitcase to find
oddments from around the house, a spoon, a pair of gloves, a
key.

And there - things from my own room.

A red pen, a stapler, a dusty bottle of pink sand.

I stared at these things, entranced by her choices, the fact of
them imbuing my worthless tat with an importance I did not
know they had deserved. Were her choices arbitrary, or did
they contain a message? Did the flotsam of my life carry more
weight than I thought, and, by association, did this mean that I
was, perhaps, a little less weightless than I felt? I gathered
them up and brought them home, arranging them on the floor
of my room.

Nightly, I returned to view her harvest of things, sifting my possessions from hers, a back-and-forth conversation, a rhythmic tide of give and take that we never mentioned at breakfast.

When she left, across my floor lay a mosaic of every pilfered thing. As each new object had appeared I had added it to the whole; the pencil sharpener nestled into a hair brush, a wooden egg spooned by a scarf, the blue copybook weighted by a thimble. Between and around these chosen objects I had tapped out soft lines of sand so that each was joined to the next. Our gathered things lay in a stilled dance, symmetrically balanced to create a whole message. A message whose meaning never did come clear, but the fact of it kept me quiet company on my move toward adulthood.

Shaping the World Line by Line

by Sharon J. Clark

I paint lines on roads and buildings. People adopt pitying looks when I tell them what I do for a living, but I don't care. I've found a way to use paint and brushes to put food on my table. How many fine art graduates can claim that? Only one contemporary of mine as far as I know, and she paints portraits of pet dogs. Me? I help people in times of stress. That cheerful yellow line you followed to navigate the maze of corridors from the hospital reception to the X-ray department – that's my handiwork. You can thank me later.

The need to be creative has not deserted me though. On evenings when the tide is chasing the horizon and the wind is holding its breath, I embrace the white sandy beach as my canvas. First, I walk the high tide mark collecting flotsam spat from the belly of the sea. A bike wheel twisted and warped. Plastic tubing shaped into gnarled bones. I gather nature's gifts as well. Seaweed and shells. Pebbles of all shapes and sizes. Sometimes a hag stone with a water-eroded cavity. With these treasures, I set to work, positioning each item with careful consideration. Then I begin to create lines in the sand. Some are straight, intersecting at angles both acute and obtuse. Some are as wavy as the surface of the distant sea. And some form concentric circles around specific objects. I love the spherical floats escaped from fishing boats. Sitting in the centre of my circles they become bright coloured worlds sending soundless ripples across the sand.

These creations are my own personal Zen gardens. As I work, I whisper words of peace and joy and harmony into their souls. Sometimes I name them, but I never share this information because names are power. When I am done, I climb the cliff and observe the beach walkers with their dogs, the families with dancing children, the strolling couples with hands entwined in the delight of new romance. Most fail to notice my art, but some will stop to admire the unity of lines and objects. They breathe in the salt sea air, filling their lungs with my words of blessing. Rarely do they look up to see me sitting on top of the cliff, but if they do I wave and softly whisper, "You can thank me later."

We Are All Magicians When We Need to Be

by Tina M. Edwards

It's early February and the whelk eggs on the beach have clumped together like a ball of lumpy porridge, creating a temporary tattoo in the wet sand. I watch his podgy hands lunge at the knobbly mass, like one of those grabbers in the arcade we'd visited earlier. The arcade with the Octonaut submarine outside, not Peppa Pig at the end of the promenade. The one where he'd sobbed uncontrollably as the grabber dropped the raggedy monkey ... right at the last moment. And despite my heart doing flip flops looking at his forlorn face, I couldn't magic another pound coin from behind my ears. I am exhausted, drained of every ounce of energy I may never have had, unable to imagine how our lives will carry on another day without her.

Later that night we place the lumpy porridge in a cold-water bath, watching it bob up and down on ripples created by a dripping tap, adding salt flakes from the condiment rack in the kitchen, praying the eggs will somehow survive. Much, much later, we place them under his pillow, safe, warm, and hidden from the Lego dinosaur who hasn't eaten for thousands of years. The smell of the sea fills our nostrils through frayed cotton pillowcases as we drift off to sleep. When we wake the next morning, the smell has gone, replaced by a large wet patch where his head has lain, the dinosaur more stealth-like than either of us could have imagined. He yawns, rubbing sleepy dust from his eyes and I watch his tongue acrobat around lip and cheeks, salt hitting his hypothalamus like a drug, dopamine rushing through veins like a train. He gives me the biggest smile yet; one I haven't seen in a long time.

Today, like every other day, we'll revisit the circus. I'll make sure there is candyfloss, popcorn, and more lumpy porridge ... but this time, there will be gold-coloured chocolate pounds. Magicked from behind ears.

The Silent Highwayman

by E.E. Parkhouse

They say an elephant once walked upon the frozen River Thames under Blackfriars Bridge. I'm not sure I believe them but unnatural things happen by this river every day. I say this because there is a piece of vertebra next to my boot. A shattered femur is prodding a cracked, silver shell a few steps away. That chip of rib is so small it must belong to an animal but the slice of jawbone poking out from beneath the rusty leaf is undoubtedly human and still has some teeth. A congregation of ancient victims rules the world below us, their bones trodden into the dark to keep us in the light.

There is a young girl of around nine plodding over the rubble of lives, her father trailing behind looking at a phone. Her blonde hair splinters the winter sun so it shines radiantly from her head. She is picking up the clay smoking pipes that turn up everywhere, like sand embedded in your skin, and is clutching them like hidden secrets. She picks up yet another grey tube and greedily adds it to her ascetic collection. Although that one is actually a little finger. She looks up at me and smiles as she passes and I smile encouragingly right back.

When the little girl and her father have gone and the crunchy skittering, like dominoes finally falling, of others' footsteps has faded and left only the irregular slosh of the river edge, I turn out my pockets and let the shards of bone fall. A few fractures of pulverised skull and one or two toe joints. They settle among their ancestors (and the pieces from yesterday), intertwining historical lines, where they'll settle endlessly, being abluted twice daily by the purifying tide.

They say an elephant once walked upon the frozen River Thames under Blackfriars Bridge. I'm not sure I believe them but unnatural things happen by this river every day.

Unholy Sonnet

by Terry O'Brien

"A fever can bring that head, which yesterday carried a crown of gold, five foot towards a crown of glory, as low as his own foot, today."

– from *Devotions*, John Donne.

With shit, literally,

                  p

                    o

                      u

                        r

                        i

                          n

                            g

                                      out of him,
near panics. When will the fear (*it's a symptom
of something serious*), and self-pity, kick in?
Still, would-be poet thinks of penning some
"personal" verse on the curse. Post it online,
where, maybe, some praise its fine, if gritty
delineation of its "feels". But, to his relief,
the excremental rush s-l-o-w-s, then congeals.
His belief the cause some rancid prawn. So,
bum still-burning, draws a line in the sand,
moves silently on. Leaves the earnest
"confessional" to whiny, hypochondriacal
mess. Or, far more poignant, some poor soul's
elegiac take on fatal illness or on heartache.

Hand in Hand on the Edge

by Nicole Durman

It's tough–
the skin of a frequent self-harmer.
My tiny crooked scythe finally breaks
through edges puffed with lidocaine,
a cat's spine: all of it a bluff. It isn't
enough. Sharp
intakes, wince, razorblade
slices of quince. Gauze sups.
Again and again,
suture, interrupted–
wrap wrap tie,
wrap wrap tie–
a nursery rhyme.

*Her mum is here, warily counting each superficial tally. Did she
read her stories? Hold her on her lap and imbue her ears with
owls? Sliding fingers through soft little girl hair, making it shiny
with the tears and sweat of motherhood?*

Rubber fingers close
the rift, clinical, dumb–
working the tools. Sterile
runcible spoon.

This must be open heart surgery, surely.

Ignoring
a forehead itch. Rugby ball
stitch. Nearly done.
She glances from her phone
screen, counts the six. Neat
in a row. The work is good,
the patient is worthy. She knows
she'll do it again.

The Other Poet Drives a Black Mercedes

by Órfhlaith Foyle

The other poet drives a black Mercedes, knows historians and sea swimmers and remarks from that Portumna on, the land goes back in time, closes in, grows dark and stays quiet.

I am the second poet, sipping water hoping that our conversation won't die a death from my shyness, and I can see the landscape gnarl itself into dark green and whirring down my window, I smell rank sweet ditchwater. House windows flash the black shine of shadow and sun. I wonder if I shall spot anyone from another century. There are farming sheds standing still from the seventeen hundreds.

Cows turn their big faces and I afraid of how life goes on until we die. All those dead tucked into the ground as the ancient Mercedes purrs by.

'The Normans are coming soon,' the other poet announces so we head towards Thomastown.

The land grows bright green in the Norman fields of the South-East and Thomastown is seventeen centuries old and older as is Grenan, a 'Sunny Place' in which the other poet's black Mercedes parks.

His friend, the artist, lives here.

The artist's house is pale blue and cut in two. One half is down and the other half up where the artist's ex-wife lives and it oversees the small in-between courtyard full of rusting iron, bicycles, an old rowing boat, and a pear and an apple tree.

He insists he comes from Vikings. No, from the knobbled dark bog, the other poet says.

The artist shows me how to pluck a pear from its bough, my hand under its belly, once ripe it will drop into my palm. I bite into it. The flesh is hardly soft yet sweet.

Mind the dog dirt, the artist warns me.

We say goodbye and while the other poet drives the Mercedes, the dark sunlight lays over the land with its last warmth, recycled from all those centuries ago, and the world is miasma and all the others of us are still here.

Snow Hill to Selfridges

by Alan Summers

As if in sand, footsteps appear at the wrong end of a train station: They run the electronic message gauntlet telling half their own stories.

Successful, the next station becomes Moor Street, full of Christmas, and its Grade II listed Edwardian era *Centenary Lounge;* its vibrations *Art Deco.* Barely impossible to leave, or linger longer, a line in the sand is crossed, so steps shift further into the mission. Beyond the ticket barrier, the Dalek decals call out in B&W and silver halide ionic crystals, all atomic number 47.

There's a popular Christmas tree, with excellent needle retention, generously lush, with dark needles, pulling away from imagination, but it's not there yet.

Streets of occasional hints of elusive green, red, blue, and tangerine, until an Italian restaurant spills out into an entrance that fills with bauble after bauble into hibernal cheer. It's almost a wardrobe, without shrugging past big winter coats, merely coaxing forwards and inwards. The whole place sparkles, as if, as if . . .

Evening closes out the light of day, and mile after mile, before toes head home, they miss out on Santa at the Big Store, though feet relax at its American Diners, and Sushi Bars. It's actually post-New Year (just), though there are still the end-embers of *Julefrokost.*

Footsteps resume the way back to Snow Hill, in name only.

Nordmann Fir
an imaginary fox
inverts sundown

Note: *Julefrokost* (Danish: "Christmas meal that lasts an entire day")

Ramblers

by Sue Norton

From the cliff they watch a man
rake spirals in sand. He's tracing
an ammonite, though soon the tide
will run up the beach and lick it clean.
Now the artist tries the unbreakable
bond of a sailor's twining Celtic knot,
though waves will wipe this symbol too.

A shame the passing ramblers say.
Their tongues scoop and excavate
Mr Whippy's creamy swirls, careful
to mop each trickling drip. Munching
remains of waffle cones, they walk

to where the coast path turns
and when it dips, it swallows them.

St Mary's

by Gary Krishna

I drag my feet through the winter slush. It's Christmas Eve, not that that matters to me, could be any day of the year, I'd be doing the same shit. The only differentiating factor is the cold. I'm very cold. At least I can get some shelter behind the giant church amongst the ancient graves.

I'm unpacking my kit with meticulous care, a one mil, a spoon, some clean water that I collected from the Queens Head toilet on the way here, two lighters, one with a flint the other with gas. And one candle I've stolen from the church on a previous visit.

Ironic I'm behind the church again, as I'm praying that I can get a vein, praying the gear's good, praying for the sickness to go away, praying, praying, praying. Pleading, pleading.

I put one grimy hand into my once white sports sock and pull out the answer to the cold, the sickness, the immediate future: the little baggy. Please God ….

I pour the powder onto the spoon, add water and citric, light the candle with the two lighters, and cook it into a milky brown liquid. I draw it up into the syringe, flick the barrel to release the bubbles, and proceed to try and inject in the well bruised and used sites in varying parts of my body.

I'm getting desperate as the cold is making it even more difficult, my veins all but collapsed from years of abuse. Dear God, please, please ….

The liquid is now becoming congealed with my own blood; the chances of me getting this hit in are reducing rapidly.

After a few more attempts I concede defeat, stand up and pull down my stinking tracksuit bottoms and shorts, and stab the needle into my bum cheek, forcing the congealed blood and heroin deep into my buttocks.

Please God make it work, let me feel it, at least stop the sickness. 'Fuck!' I scream into the dark night. I slump down against the church wall, hopeless, as the angelic sound of the church choir singing *Silent Night, Holy Night* floats into the graveyard.

I hum along, "all is calm, all is bright."

It Was Seeing the Leading Actor Shaving

by Rose Lennard

It was seeing the leading actor shaving

drawing the blade down his young cheek,
peeling away the lather like fleece
from the flank of a summer ram,

that reminded me of him, how he was
in our early days, his face soft and smooth
and soap-scented each morning as our lips

met; and he came into my dream that night,
ten years after our separation, we stepped
together into the stillest of shallow waters,

and I remember how we never fought,
how I thought unrippled was better
than breaking waves; and in my dream

the sea is vanishing like water
draining from a bathtub, until we are far out,
ankle deep, and nothing to plunge into.

Môn Mam

by Katrina Moinet

language

unplanned future

unfamiliar map

terr-i-toire

someone else's

she-island

my native i land

my ynys is not

île de mon père

hardened place

hen vaterland

who owns this

pinpointed

came mum of mine

môn mam cymru

out to sea

my eye's gaze

island encircles

il me manque cette

far from home

arcipelago largo

de ma patrie

pas trop loin

lost i land

an island

no woman's

my grain notion

her loss

sans reference

my hat that's

wherever I lay

O, look how my

commence avec

faraway once i

grains of sable

toes rub against

my feet sink in

as i walk this aisle

my island solitaire

môn is mine

Curl and Blacken

by Will Gillingham

It was on the third day that it became clear that Mother wasn't coming. The post hadn't arrived on account of the storm and Father had driven to the post office in the village in the end, the car slopping over leaves and dirt and odd things the wind had blown up from the beach. You could tell something was wrong when he got back because he parked where Mother parks and his smile looked Pritt sticked to his cheeks. We sat in the kitchen for some time, Father looking like he did that time I left my disposable camera on the train, me and Benjamin listening to the sand buzzing against the windows. In the end Father told us to get our wellies on. We trudged down to the beach, hoods up on our raincoats and cords pulled tight to fend off the tiny stings, and when we got there the plan was to collect as much driftwood as possible. Father went one way, me and Benjamin the other, and the lines we made from dragging back the driftwood looked like spaghetti. We bundled it all up in one spot and Father crouched over it with his lighter, whispering to the plastic, magicking a flame into existence. Eventually a small fire took hold and we all huddled close with our arms around each other, backs to the wind, to keep it from going out. It wriggled around the wood like a snail, and after a while Father took a letter from his pocket and threw it right into the middle. We watched it curl and blacken in silence, and when it was gone, none of us felt like moving. So that's where we stayed, me, Benjamin and Father, shielding the flame until the light fled from the sky.

Between the Kettle and the Stars: a Line in the Sand

by John Gallas

'If God had given her water, she'd have been a great swimmer' –
Sudanese proverb

We stop at Umm Lahayy. The stars hang fire,
like boats in books that shine along the sea
in search of God. The jabanah. The tea.
The tentflaps flap. We lie back to admire
what Heaven is, so far from us. A curl
of dung-smoke. Ayub yawns. The camels shift
and sigh. I snooze with proper awe, adrift
in His great vastness. 'I can swim,' says Durl,
softly ... out of nothing ... 'Like a fish.'
I smile, unroll my rug, and say a prayer.
Forgive our sins – I guess there's room up there.
The sand-dunes look like spellbound waves. I wish
my friends good night ... dreams and doubts and hope ...
a little lie ... the world turns ... God can cope.

Drawn Together

by Gareth Leaney

Scoop. Scoop. Forward. Scoop, scoop, forward…

Yaku's practiced hand easily slid the bone tool under the surface and flipped the rust-red soil away, revealing another patch of yellow. Inch by inch, one scoop to the left then one to the right, Yaku scraped his newest design across the desert.

After a while he stopped and wiped his brow with his cloth cap. The brutal sun that baked the desert sand threatened to bake Yaku as he worked. He looked behind him: the pale yellow furrow narrowed to a point on the horizon. Ahead, empty red desert stretched in every direction. A small crowd had gathered on the hill that rose in the distance, watching him work and fanning themselves gently with maize leaves. Yaku scanned the blurry shapes - as usual, Saywa was not among them. He turned back to his work.

Scoop. Scoop. Forward.

The shamans had sipped on their cactus tea and muttered that the gods would be pleased. The Great Killer Whale, the Jaguar, the Condor would look down on their effigies and smile, the shamans said. A good harvest was sure. But there was only one divine being whose favour mattered to Yaku. And 'his' Saywa was not so easily impressed.

His early efforts, stick-etched in the soil, barely raised an eyebrow. Of course, Yaku had chuckled; a woman like Saywa had standards!

But then she laughed at his Spider. 8 legs, 150 feet, and it got him nowhere.

She shook her head at his Great Whale. Maybe the tail wasn't quite right? He had never seen one himself, after all.

Yaku drew flowers, and trees, a vast curly-tailed monkey, a diving pelican. He drew and drew. He would not stop until Saywa was his, if it meant filling the wide red desert.

Sometimes he wondered what visitors might think of his drawings. If they remained here, marking the sand for years to come, would his grandchildren or their grandchildren wonder where they came from? What stories might they invent to explain them?

Yaku chuckled. What other reason could there possibly be?!

He looked up. Saywa had joined the crowd! He risked a wave.

Yaku had a good feeling about this one.
A hummingbird fluttered around a clump of desert flowers. He studied it for a moment, the delicate wings, the slender beak.

He picked up his tool again and began to draw.

The Scaregull

by Josh Thorpe

Well hi there Bournemouthians, and heck, what a nice sandy beach you got goin' on right here. Dorset coast and all that. Yep I sure do appreciate the vibe of all these sweeping curves and breezy days. Like to go for a swim cuz you know my hair looked great—from the saltwater? Regular Matthew McConaughey over here! Why can't they bottle that stuff? I'd buy that goop in a second back home in Texarkana. No sea there.

I will say this: You could do something on this uh, seagull situation? Like, there I am, sitting on this sweet beach, plum pleased by the pretty picture, you know, looking at the waves, getting half-mesmerized by the vibe of it all. And then this dang seagull come along, disturbing the peace, yelling at me who knows what nonsense, try to steal my chips, and practically do its business on my shirt.

I mean, it don't in-actual-fact do its business on my shirt. Not this time, anyway, though we both know they *would*. It's an indignity and a pain in the butt, if I'm honest. They say to be hit by bird scat is good luck? Sure don't feel that way at the time.

Now, I'm an animal lover in the end, so I don't begrudge these fowl their actions. You look up at one a them catching a thermal, they look perfectly still, at one with the wind, a wind-gull salt-air system, you know. And they do resemble some kind of prehistoric beast, if you get the right angle that is. Frightful things gulls, hahaha!

So I ain't saying, like, 'cull the gull', or, I mean maybe put a few more spikes up on those gazebos or whatever, and I'd like to see some better bins the darn things can't get into all the time? Can't be good for a bird's diet, after all, eatin' piles of chips and kidney pie.

Anyway, so if you go down there to Boscombe or whatever, don't freak out if y'all see like a driftwood effigy type dude built up in the sand there. That's just my scaregull—like a scarecrow for gulls? I don't say it'll work, but.

Yeah so, I practically just gave those dudes my chips anyway and I think they started to kind of like me in the end. And they were like, nice hair, Tex. Prehistoric chuckleheads hahaha!

Authors' Bios & Judges' Comments on the Winning Entries

(arranged in alphabetical order of the authors' first names)

Alan Summers

Bio   Alan (South West of England, UK) was deeply inspired by Birmingham (UK), a gloriously friendly city. A love of Christmas, and Birmingham, evolved into this hybrid genre called 'haibun' (prose + haiku). He is founder of Call of the Page, which mentors and supports writers worldwide.

Judge's Comments on Snow Hill to Selfridges – page 59

You'll find poetic language and atmospheric qualities in the prose here, hinting at a journey that is both physical and metaphorical. The note explaining *Julefrokost* adds a layer of cultural richness, enhancing the reader's understanding of the narrative and further immersing them in the writer's unique world.

Alice E. Bennett

Bio   Based in the Wiltshire town of Swindon, Alice's writing style draws heavily on vibrant environments and subtle humour to reflect modern challenges to our collective sense of place and belonging. She regularly produces content for her website, *My Housemate's a Mermaid*, alongside book reviews for Reedsy Discovery.

Judge's Comments on How the Dressmaker of Bournemouth Feeds Her Family – page 13

A well-crafted, thought-provoking story with good attention to detail and glittered with humour, prompting the reader to reflect on themes of self-expression, transformation, and authenticity, while considering the choices we make in presenting ourselves to the world.

Antoine Cassar

Bio   Antoine is a London-born Maltese poet. *Forty Days*, a cycle of poems on childhood trauma and walking as self-therapy, was awarded the 2018 Malta National Book Prize. *Passport*, a poetic 'anti-passport' for all peoples, has been adapted by theatre groups in Europe, North America and Australia. www.antoinecassar.net

Judge's Comments on Island Seeker – page 33

This poem uses an engaging conceit to link cityscape with seascape 'in an ocean of stone'. An interesting exploration of what it means to have direction in life.

❖

Carol Maxwell

Bio   Carol is a daughter, sister, wife, friend and retired audiometrist based in Blenheim, New Zealand. Also, a poet published in several local and international magazines and anthologies. When she's not shepherding words, she is reading them, working in creative fibres, outdoors gardening, hiking, or messing about in boats.

Judge's Comments on Woman Standing on Her Bathroom Scales – page 20

Clever use of presentation on the page to suggest the fluctuating dial on the bathroom scales . Both painful and funny in equal measure, this is an inventive exploration of the social baggage women carry.

Charles Kitching

Bio Charles has written since childhood. He studied
Philosophy at University, followed by a MA in
Representation and Modernity. He's had careers in
Universities, in contemporary circus/physical theatre,
historic conservation and running a GP practice's
dispensary. Apart from writing, his main interests are in
photography, art and history.

*Judge's Comments on No Matter Which Way the Wind Blows –
page 21*

The writer demonstrates storytelling skill in weaving
together two perspectives, drawing the reader into a
reflection on the intricate connections between past and
present, privilege and struggle, and the resilience of the
human spirit in times of turmoil and upheaval.

Craig Smith

Bio Craig's work has appeared on Writers Rebel, Magma,
MIRonline, iamb, Atrium, and The North. He was a winner
of Poetry Archive Now WordWise 2022, was longlisted for
the Brotherton Poetry Prize, and is cited as a rising star in
the 2023 London Independent Story Prize anthology.
Blog: clattermonger.com Twitter: @clattermonger.

Judge's Comments on Castle – page 18

This poem appeals because it resonates way beyond its
subject-matter, described with beauty and tenderness. It's
also a poem about connecting, building relationships and
the ephemeral nature of a shared moment.

Cristín Leach

Bio Cristín is the author of the memoir *Negative Space* (2022) and the experimental art writing collection *From Ten till Dusk* (2023). Her short fiction and personal essays have been published in Winter Papers, and her art criticism has appeared in *The Sunday Times Culture (Ireland)* since 2003.

Judge's Comments on Unstuck – page 45

The first line of *Unstuck* is a deftly written, unusual opening hook. The symbolism of the fragile limpet echoes the protagonist's own journey of shedding past burdens and embracing new beginnings - beautiful flash fiction about the intricacies of womanhood and the resilience that comes with facing challenges head-on.

Dave Martin

Bio Dave, poet and historian, lives and writes in Dorset. His work has been published in a variety of papers and journals. This haiku was composed whilst paddling along the shoreline. His latest chapbook *Running with Poets* imagines famous poets visiting and writing about parkrun. He tweets @DaveMartin46

Judge's Comments on [Untitled] – page 44

An engaging haiku with well-selected sensory vocabulary. It brings to life the sensation of tidal white froth ebbing and flowing on a beach in a way that invites the reader in to share the scene.

David Longstaff

Bio   David began writing stories two years ago. He has been shortlisted and a winner in six UK competitions. His dark humour is always present. He is an inch shorter than he was, has size 12 feet and his enlarged prostrate is currently being treated. He no longer owns a dog.

Judge's Comments on A Fishy Tale – page 35

A captivating, intense and suspenseful story playing with imageries usually found in crime fiction to maintain tension. The unexpected plot twists keep the reader on the edge of their seat and the haunting imagery of the 'mermaid' being dragged into the sea, amidst chaos and confusion, is both heart-breaking and compelling.

E.E. Parkhouse

Bio   E.E. is a History with Creative Writing undergraduate. With a love of both the written and spoken word, she is fascinated by strong female characters in both history and fiction. Originally from Hampshire, she now lives in London. This is her first published piece.

Judge's Comments on The Silent Highwayman – page 53

An eerie, haunting post-apocalyptic story, with imagery of a desolate world of human remains and macabre beauty. The elephant walking on the frozen Thames adds a touch of surrealism and mystery to the narrative, inviting the reader to ponder the fragility of civilization and the remnants in its wake.

Elliot Chester

Bio   Elliot has written, illustrated and self-published a children's rhyme and colouring book, *Catch an Echo*. He has been published in numerous zines and anthologies, including; WrittenOff Publishing, Ink Spill and Village Voices, to name a few. His passion is to read and write flash fiction, poetry and prose.

Judge's Comments on The Crescendo at Blue Beach, Gaza – page 41

I was enraptured by this important, timely story and its intricate, haunting imagery. The use of music as a metaphor for the narrator's emotions and experiences adds a depth and complexity to the narrative, as each symbol and note reveal the truth about the effects of conflict and trauma.

Gareth Leaney

Bio   As a science teacher and as a writer, Gareth's work questions why things are the way they are and why people do the things they do. *Drawn Together* was inspired by the mysterious Nazca Lines in the Peruvian desert, and the crazy things we do for love.

Judge's Comments on Drawn Together – page 67

Employing vivid imagery and immersive language - the harsh desert, the sweltering sun, the meticulous process of making art in the sand – builds atmosphere, leaving room for imagination and contemplation, encouraging the reader to reflect on the deeper meanings behind Yaku's art and his quest for love and recognition.

Gary Krishna

Bio   Gary, lead artist for The Outsiders Project, found his passion for writing and performing late in life. He tours prisons, conducting workshops and sharing his work, bringing his self-disclosure, creativity and connection to those attending. His dedication and passion for arts in recovery inspires others to find purpose.

Judge's Comments on St Mary's – page 61

The storytelling was both heartbreaking and haunting, capturing the character's inner dialogue and prayers for solace during addiction. The juxtaposition of the character's plea to a higher power for relief against the background of an angelic choir, creates a powerful contrast, reflecting the inner conflict and struggle for redemption.

Georgina Titmus

Bio   Georgina Titmus is a 60-something poet and carer, living in Cornwall. She's been published in: The Journal, South, Orbis, The Frogmore Papers, The Moth, Fenland Poetry Journal, Full House Literary, The Pomegranate & others. She writes with the aid of a 1980s' electronic typewriter, made in the former GDR.

Judge's Comments on Body Found on Seafront – page 43

A well-crafted and structured poem which uses white space on the page to intensify the atmosphere of mystery. The fragmentation of the narrative is powerful.

Helen Chambers

Bio   Helen is a fair-weather sea swimmer who wishes she could dance. She writes flash and short fiction, and you can read some of her other publications here: https://helenchamberswriter.wordpress.com/writing/

Judge's Comments on Changeling – page 31

This fiction contrasts the protagonist's struggles on land and their liberation in the sea. The seamless blend of reality and fantasy creates a sense of wonder and intrigue, achieved through the lyrical writing style, thematic depth and captivating world-building.

Helen Kay

Bio   Helen's second pamphlet, *This Lexia & Other Languages* (v.press) arrived in 2020. She curates a platform for dyslexic poets: dyslexiapoetry.co.uk. She was the winner of the 2023 Ironbridge and Repton Prizes and shortlisted for the Live Canon Pamphlet Prize.

Judge's Comments on On Hilbre Island, West Kirby – page 30

Imagery choices makes this poem dynamic with 'bobbles of grey seals' and 'a braille of shells'. Synaesthesia invites the reader into an interesting sensory experience of sipping the sun and tasting flowers.

Helen Jane Campbell

Bio   Helen writes magical short stories for grown-ups. Her protagonists often feel out of place in their lives or bodies, a discomfort which leads to unexpected adventure. Helen lives in sunny Worthing, Sussex, with her girlfriend Rachel. Business Expert Press published her non-fiction book: *Founders, Freelancers & Rebels* (2021).

Judge's Comments on Weather House – page 23

A delightful and memorable read with an imaginative and whimsical nature. The exploration of yearning for connection and escape from routine duties is sympathetically depicted and the story is engaging, thought-provoking, and beautifully written.

Henry Edwards

Bio   Henry comes from Brentwood in Essex, but now lives with his family in Bremen, Germany. Assisted-dying is a sad theme, but one which needs to be addressed. His own mother died in somewhat 'undignified' circumstances, which could have been different, had laws allowed. Hence the story…

Judge's Comments on Might Love End Life – page 27

A raw and honest portrayal of love and loss, the vivid descriptions of physical decline of the loved one, juxtaposed with happy memories tied to the coast, evoke a deep sense of sadness and longing. The story subtly refers to the landscape to deepen the emotional impact.

Joanna Bury

Bio Joanna has a passion to write stories about the climate and nature crises, and about environmental activism. She explores human responses to the increasingly difficult circumstances we all face on our one and only home, planet Earth. She recently completed her first novel, *New Words For Rain* on these themes

Judge's Comments on Rising – page 37

Rising intricately weaves themes of defiance, resilience, and acceptance in the face of adversity. The gradual build-up of tension and uncertainty as the couple refuse to evacuate – the nuanced portrayal of their inner thoughts and dialogue captures the complexities of their decision to stay, revealing stubbornness, fear, and nostalgia.

John Gallas

Bio John, Aotearoa poet, 30 books, mostly published by Carcanet (www.carcanet.co.uk). See website www.johngallaspoetry.co.uk Poem inspired by the Proverb [from an old charity-shop book, *Wisdom of the World: Proverbs* (1951)].

Judge's Comments on Between the Kettle and the Stars: a Line in the Sand – page 66

An engaging portrayal of a shared experience which weaves in other voices in its telling. Interesting blend of imagery connected to divine and mortal worlds.

Josh Thorpe

Bio   Josh is a writer, visual artist, and musician from Canada, now living in Glasgow. His artwork has been exhibited internationally, he has published a few articles and poems in Canada, and he hosts a radio show on ResonanceFM. He has just completed his first novel. Learn more at www.joshthorpe.com.

Judge's Comments on The Scaregull – page 69

The colourful and vibrant personality of the narrator shines through in their Texan drawl and casual observations, creating a sense of familiarity and connection with the audience. Overall, *The Scaregull* is a delightful and engaging narrative that combines wit, insight, and a love for the quirks of seaside life.

Julia Rapp

Bio   Julia is a poet/songwriter living in Brooklyn, New York and working as a writer. She has been featured in Birdcoat Quarterly, Chaotic Merge, 45th Parallel, Angle and others. She received her MFA in Creative Writing from Saint Mary's College of California. On social media: @jujujulife, and Spotify under Julia Rapp.

Judge's Comments on To My Future Ex-Husband, With Love – page 25

Appealingly quirky in its concept and choice of imagery, this poem has an arresting voice. Undoubtedly funny, but there's a subtle poignancy to the consideration of relationships and motherhood.

Katrina Moinet

Bio   Katrina is Globe Soup Short Story prize-winner. Katrina's work is published in Mslexia, Raw Lit, The PostGrad Journal, Ffosfforws, Firmament, and longlisted in Mslexia, New Writers, and Fish competitions. Their debut collection's forthcoming with Hedgehog Press. Katrina hosts Blue Sky open mic & co-runs Gwyl Môn Writing Festival.   @KMoinetwrites   katrinamoinet.com

Judge's Comments on Môn Mam – page 64

Interestingly structured, the poem's stanzas float on the page like islands in the sea – an archipelago. The multilingual representation helps to present the theme of identity.

Kim Waters

Bio   Kim was inspired to write *Blue Hospital Gown* after her mother spent time in a hospital with a serious infection. Kim lives in Melbourne, Australia, and enjoys writing poetry and short stories. Her poems have appeared in The Australian, The Shanghai Literary Review, Cordite, Wells Street Journal and Marble.

Judge's Comments on Blue Hospital Gown – page 26

The simplicity of language and structure helps to illuminate the personal importance of the subject-matter. An elegy for life, loss and memory, this poem really pulls at the heartstrings.

Laurie Keim

Bio   Laurie is a prize-winning Australian poet who has won the Val Vallis Poetry Award among others. Recent volumes of poetry are *Writing On Air* (2015), *Future of Music* (2020) and *Between the Mirror and the Bed* (2024 microfictions and poems) - highly acclaimed for their uplifting cadences and piercing insights.

Judge's Comments on Ghost Crabs – page 15

A beautifully expressed 'in the moment' poem which describes a natural occurrence that carries a wider message about the cyclical patterns of communication.

Michael Pettit

Bio   Michael is a South African artist – a painter. His short stories have appeared in The Barcelona Review, The Bookends Review, WestWord Prize (3rd Prize), Parracombe Prize anthology, and Hammond House Prize anthology (Editor's International Choice award) where he also won 1st Prize for his song lyrics.

Judge's Comments on Tango – page 39

With an unusual, striking opening, this story captures a moment of tension and disconnect between the couple dexterously, with subtle gestures and movements speaking volumes about their relationship. Overall, the narrative is rich in detail and emotion, inviting reflection on the complexities of human relationships and communication.

Neil Douglas

Bio   Neil worked as a GP and Community Paediatrican in London's East End. His poetry has been published in magazines and anthologies in the UK, North America and Hong Kong. He has recently graduated with an MA in Creative and Life Writing from Goldsmiths University of London.

Judge's Comments on Cheese Sandwich – page 12

A satisfyingly satirical prose poem. It wittily juxtaposes the filming of a perfume advertisement with a less glamorous reality. High end fragrance meets sweating cheese sandwich.

Nicole Durman

Bio   Nicole is an American and British poet and nurse based in Somerset. She has been published in the book, *Balancing on a Bootheel: New Voices in Poetry from Southeast Missouri*, and is a current member of the Fire River Poetry group.

Judge's Comments on Hand in Hand on the Edge – page 56

This poem illuminates a sensitive topic with some powerful language and imagery choices. The depiction of childhood in this poem is particularly striking.

Oonagh Montague

Bio   Oonagh is based in Cork, Ireland. A former journalist and editor of Arts Ireland, her fiction is included in Winter Papers (Curlew Editions) and the anthology Cork Stories (Doire Press). *Harvest of Things* is a moment when life hints at a pattern we try to decipher.

Judge's Comments on Harvest of Things – page 47

A nuanced exploration of vulnerability, perception, and connection, depicting the adult world through the lens of a child witnessing a woman with kleptomania. The imagery of stolen items forming a symbolic mosaic highlights the interplay between personal possessions and emotional weight, raising questions about identity, value, and relationships.

Órfhlaith Foyle

Bio   Órfhlaith is a poet, writer and radio dramatist living in Galway, Ireland. She has published one poetry collection *Red Riding Hood's Dilemma* (Arlen House) and three collections of short fiction. Her most recent, *Three Houses in Rome* was published by Doire Press (September 2023).

Judge's Comments on The Other Poet Drives a Black Mercedes – page 57

A captivating story, leaving a lingering impression of the transient yet enduring essence of life, beautifully encapsulated in the shifting light and shadows of the landscape. The themes of time, history, and mortality are woven seamlessly, drawing the reader into a contemplative reflection on life and continuity.

Partridge Boswell

Bio   Author of the 2024 Fool for Poetry Prize-winning chapbook *Levis Corner House* and Grolier Prize-winning collection *Some Far Country*, Partridge is co-founder of Bookstock Literary Festival and teaches at Vallum Society for Education in Arts & Letters in Montreal. He troubadours widely with the poetry/music group Los Lorcas and lives with his family in Vermont.

Judge's Comments on Georgic – page 16

This poem gives modern relevance to the pastoral. With well-placed religious overtones, a life lost leads to a consideration of death, humankind and the cycle of life.

Robin Muers

Bio   Robin has always been interested in contemporary poetry. Recent favourites include John Burnside and Ada Limón. After retirement – now a long time ago! – he made further attempts to write some verse of his own.

Judge's Comments on I Witness Creation – page 11

A thought-provoking consideration of how adults can spoil the magic of a child's game. Described in a modern mock-heroic style, this poem is powerfully observed.

Roger Hare

Bio   Herefordshire poet Roger writes from what distracts him - things overheard, observed and felt - and particularly enjoys the stimulation offered by works of art. He's published in several anthologies and magazines, is a five-time competition prize-winner, and Best of the Net and Pushcart nominated. He's found on TwitterX @RogerHare6

Judge's Comments on Paul Klee Said, 'Take a Line for a Walk' – page 29

An exciting and visually pleasing poem which uses the concrete form to explore Paul Klee's concept of 'a line going for a walk'. It also starts an interesting conversation about what it means to stay within the lines.

Rose Lennard

Bio   Sometimes poems take Rose by surprise, like this unexpected association when watching a film sparking a dream image which stayed with her and wanted to be written about. Poems help to process life events, even years later, and seem to work best when the subconscious gets a say.

Judge's Comments on It Was Seeing the Leading Actor Shaving – page 63

A simple image takes the speaker back into memory and a past relationship. Thought-provoking use of imagery to show communication in a relationship as being either 'unrippled' or 'breaking waves'.

Sharon J. Clark

Bio   Based in Milton Keynes, Sharon has been published in various anthologies and online literary magazines, including Still Point Arts Quarterly, Blink Ink and Reflex Fiction. She has self-published two poetry collections and is working on a short story collection. Read more at www.sharonjclark.co.uk

Judge's Comments on Shaping the World Line By Line – page 49

This story invites readers to appreciate the beauty of the everyday. I enjoyed the nature imagery and the unique perspective of the protagonist. Overall, I appreciated the theme of finding joy and meaning in everyday acts of creativity and kindness.

Sue Norton

Bio   Sue's work has appeared in various anthologies and magazines, most recently in Poetry News and forthcoming in The North. The poem *Ramblers* was inspired by a video of the work of the Cornish sand artist, Tony Plant.

Judge's Comments on Ramblers – page 60

The clarity of language and careful placing of each word makes this poem sparkle. Clever continuation of imagery associated with eating: 'lick', 'munching' and 'swallows' frames this poem which is about the poignancy of a simple moment.

Terry O'Brien

Bio   Ex-college lecturer, Terry O'Brien grew up - sort of - mostly on a council estate north of London. Gained a degree in English and Philosophy during punk rock's heyday; spent a "gap" year as a hospital porter; returned to uni to complete a Masters; then began thirty plus years teaching.

Judge's Comments on Unholy Sonnet – page 55

An irreverent exploration of what it means to be a poet. Scatological humour is used to shape the poem and cleverly becomes a metaphor for the writing process itself.

Tessa Foley

Bio   Tessa's *Chalet Between Thick Ears* and *What Sort of Bird are You?* were published by Live Canon. Recently recognised in the Molecules Unlimited Poetry Competition and the Waltham Forest Poetry Prize and has been featured in Agenda, Alchemy Spoon, Finished Creatures, Ink, Sweat & Tears, Black Iris and Crank Mag.

Judge's Comments on Where All the Vibrators Go – page 34

This poem answers an unusual question with appealing tongue-in-cheek humour. It's cleverly layered to include the underlying ecological issue of how humans dispose of products.

Tina M. Edwards

Bio   Tina's flash fiction has been selected for National Flash Fiction Day Anthology 2024, long-listed by Bath Flash Fiction Award with publication, as well as being published by others. She is also a published author and poet and loves the sea, coast, and all things weird and wonderful.

Judge's Comments on We Are All Magicians When We Need to Be – page 51

The title suggests that, in times of adversity or hardship, individuals have the power to tap into their inner strength and resourcefulness to overcome challenges. The progression from sorrow and exhaustion to a moment of shared joy and connection between the characters is touching and resonant.

Will Gillingham

Bio   Will Gillingham was born in Bournemouth and studied Creative Writing at the University of Birmingham. He remembers many a windy walk on deserted winter beaches, and *Curl and Blacken* was inspired by those memories. He now lives in London.

Judge's Comments on Curl and Blacken – page 65

I was drawn to the opening line of *Curl and Blacken*, which immediately propels the reader into the narrative. The author deftly captures the sense of foreboding and unease through vivid descriptions of the stormy weather, the characters' reactions, and the desolate beach setting.

WORKSHOPS

TALKS

KIDS

ACTIVITIES

Inspiring Writers to Write

Three-day Festival

Facebook Writing Group

Year-round networking events

Informal Writing Groups

Plus more to come!

ornemouth
ing
val

DITHERING

CHAPS

Indie publisher of carefully-crafted chapbooks

In addition to Lines in the Sand, our catalogue includes:

✦ *The Sheliand by D G Herring*

✦ *Gifts of the Dark by Simon Bowden*

✦ *Going Home by Anne Peterson*

www.ditheringchaps.com

Feeling Overwhelmed With Book Marketing?

Hi, I'm Linda, a Book Marketing Consultant and Self-publishing Success Coach.

I help authors launch their books and kickstart their author careers by removing the guesswork from marketing, so they can build profitable author businesses and make an impact by writing what they love.

I can help you with:

- Book Launches
- 1:1 Book Marketing Coaching
- Backlist Marketing Audits

Schedule a free 30-minute discovery call:

www.lindaliebrand.com

At Vita Nova, our supportive community provides a safe space for individuals in recovery to express themselves, build confidence, and discover newfound passions—all FREE of charge.

Join us and experience the transformative power of the arts. Whether it's music, theatre, or creative writing, there's something here for everyone.

Know someone who might benefit from joining us? Spread the word and invite them to be a part of our community!

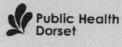

Vita Nova – New Life

2024 is a significant year for both Vita Nova and me as it's 25 years since the project began, although Vita Nova happened organically and wasn't planned!

In 1999, I was co-director of Bournemouth Theatre in Education; we were based in the Bournemouth Centre for Community Arts (BCCA), a building that has sadly been all but demolished bar what is now the Old School House. I was asked to write a secondary school, drug education piece. So I took myself to a 'dry' social club and asked if anyone would like to come to the centre and help me create a play for young people.

No one really said much, so I heard myself asking, "Do you know a play to tell people about drugs misuse …or how to take drugs safely?" and one of those present said, "There is no safe way: if there was, I wouldn't be here." His words were the beginning of my education into the disease of addiction. Thankfully, a group of recovering addicts found their way to the BCCA and together we created Vita Nova's first play *Scratchin' the Surface*.

The creation of the play had a profound effect on the group and myself as the key-working practitioner on the project. I was not prepared for the intense emotions its making would provoke. This may have been naive of me, because, of course, the nature of engaging in drama with a group of people who have been through drug addiction was bound to bring up painful situations.

However, there was something else going on, to do with 'timing'. No one could have predicted that somehow this group that emerged quite quickly – and I include myself in this – happened to be in a particular 'awakening' state of mind, almost simultaneously, that bonded us in a particularly powerful way.

The process moved quickly, as group members were like sponges, soaking up the drama medium. They didn't want to stop when the education project concluded: instead, they wanted to continue.

What Vita Nova had was, on one side, a very powerful educational message and, on the other, a 'therapeutic' engagement for the participant actors. The rest, as they say, is history. I haven't been with Vita Nova for their entire journey, although I wasn't ever too far away. As an applied drama practitioner, I have lectured at Winchester University and worked on other community projects with refugees and asylum seekers, hard to reach young people and also Gypsies and travellers.

I was invited back to Vita Nova as their Artistic Director after a long break in 2020. It's had its challenges but it is a privilege to work with such an amazingly creative and sensitive group of people. We have been on the road most of this year, with our new play about country lines, *The Wasp's Nest* and doing what Vita Nova does best - having a dialogue with young people and the wider community about the disease of addiction.

Contact us on: https://vitanova.co.uk/about/

Or email: reception@vitanova.co.uk

Sharon Mururi Coyne